THE FANTASTIC FRAME

Splat! Another Messy Sunday

BY LIN OLIVER

ILLUSTRATED BY SAMANTHA KALLIS

Grosset & Dunlap
An Imprint of Penguin Random House

For Teresa Nathanson,
my lovely art history friend—LO

For Gilbert, and a lifetime of
lovely Sunday afternoons—SK

GROSSET & DUNLAP
Penguin Young Readers Group
An Imprint of Penguin Random House LLC

Text copyright © 2016 by Lin Oliver. Illustrations copyright © 2016 by Samantha Kallis.
All rights reserved. Published by Grosset & Dunlap, an imprint of Penguin Random
House LLC, 345 Hudson Street, New York, New York 10014. GROSSET & DUNLAP
is a trademark of Penguin Random House LLC. Manufactured in China.

Library of Congress Cataloging-in-Publication Data is available.

ISBN 978-0-448-48089-3 | 10 9 8 7 6 5 4 3 2 1

PROLOGUE

Oh, hi there. I'm Tiger Brooks. I think we might have met before.

I'm here to tell you a story you're probably not going to believe. But trust me, it's all true. Even the parts that don't seem true. I know because it happened to me.

It started when my friend Luna Lopez and I paid a visit to our neighbor Viola Dots. She's the—well, let's just say *unusual* woman who lives next door with her butler, a talking orange pig named Chives. I know what you're thinking. A talking orange pig— that's a hard one to believe.

But wait, there's more. Viola has this magical, fantastic picture frame in her house. What? You're not sure magical picture frames actually exist? Well, neither was I until I fell into one. But I'm getting ahead of myself.

Viola's frame hangs on the wall in her living room. It looks like one of those fancy golden frames you'd see in a museum. And it has a gold clock on the front. When the clock on the frame strikes four, the painting inside opens up and sucks you in.

That sounds exciting, but it hasn't worked out too well for Viola Dots. Her son, David, was sucked into a painting fifty years ago and has been lost ever since. The only thing she got in return was Chives, who came flying straight out of some old painting and into her living room.

Mrs. Dots is pretty old now and still misses David like crazy, which is why Luna and I agreed to help her. Every week she paints another painting to put in the frame. And every week, we travel into the frame to look for David.

This would be totally fun except for one little detail: If we're not back from inside the painting in exactly one hour, we'll be stuck. That's right. We would have to stay in the world of art forever.

That's a good thing if you're trying to get out of doing your homework. But if you care about ever returning home, it's not so good.

I don't blame you if you don't believe me. It's a pretty wild story. So read it for yourself, and then you tell me.

Do you really think there is such a thing as a fantastic frame?

CHAPTER 1

Come on, Luna! I thought. *Where are you?*

Our wooden front porch groaned as I paced back and forth. I checked the time on my Batman watch. Luna had agreed to meet me at exactly fifteen minutes to four, but she was late. We had promised Viola Dots that we'd be at her house on time. If we were even one minute late, the magic wasn't going to work.

Luna Lopez, you're going to ruin everything!

I heard footsteps coming from inside our duplex. "Luna!" I called out. "It's about time!"

"It's not Luna," an annoying little voice said. "It's me, Maggie. I came to play with you."

Can someone please tell me why little sisters always show up at exactly the wrong time?

"I can't play with you now, squirt," I told Maggie. I tried to herd her back into the house, but the little pest wasn't budging.

"Why can't you?" Maggie stomped her foot on the porch, which made her sneakers light up.

"Are you and your new girlfriend going to visit the orange pig with the funny hat?"

I had to put an end to this conversation right now. The orange pig was a secret—only Luna and I could know he actually existed.

"Listen up, Maggie," I said. "Number one, Luna is not my girlfriend. She is a girl who happens to be a new friend. And number two, there's no such thing as an orange pig. Didn't they teach you that in preschool?"

Maggie burst out laughing. I didn't think I had said anything funny.

"Tiger, you said *number two*." She giggled. "I'm going to tell Mommy you're using bathroom words."

"Be my guest," I said. "Go tell Mom." I figured at least that would get her back into the house.

As Maggie turned and ran inside, I could hear her chanting, "Mommy, Tiger said *number two*. Tiger said *number two*."

That's four-year-olds for you. Their brains are only half-baked.

I checked my watch again. Time was running out.

Luckily, I heard Luna's footsteps clopping down the stairs. We just moved into a duplex that our families share. Luna lives in the upstairs part. This time, I knew it was her because her shoes clomp when she walks.

"Hi, Tiger," she said, like she wasn't even late at all. "My grandma made us *horchata*." She handed me a plastic cup with a frothy white liquid in it. "It's like a cinnamon toast milkshake, minus the brain freeze."

"We don't have time for refreshments," I said.

"Just taste it. It's my grandpa Arturo's recipe."

I took a sip. It was delicious.

"Your grandpa Arturo knows his stuff," I said. "But we have to hurry. The fantastic frame kicks in at four exactly, and we promised Viola we'd be there. She's counting on us."

"Okay, okay. We can drink while we walk."

Luna grabbed a flowered hat from a chair on the porch and popped it on her head. She loves to make crazy-looking hats, and this one definitely was. We raced down our driveway and headed to Viola's house. It was a crumbling old place next door to ours, with peeling blue paint and an overgrown lawn. The house was covered in cobwebs and had a spooky lookout tower on top.

We were almost at the front gate when a hand reached out and snatched my *horchata*. I turned to see a boy with bleached blond hair and braces. Before I realized that he was at least a head taller than me, I blurted out, "Hey, you! Give that back!"

"Take it easy, shrimp," the kid said. "I just want a sip."

The kid tilted the cup back and drained the whole thing in one awful gulp. Crunching my ice in his mouth, he put the cup on the ground and squashed it under his foot. Then he handed the squashed cup back to me.

"Aren't you going to introduce me to the new guy?" the boy asked Luna.

"This creep is Cooper Starr," Luna said. "He thinks he's great."

"That's why everyone calls me Super Cooper." The boy grinned, showing off his mouth full of braces.

"He lives on our street," Luna explained. "He's a very rude boy with a very small imagination."

"Hey, shrimp," Cooper said, giving me an annoying poke. "Why do you want to be friends with her? Everyone knows Luna Lopez has bugs. Don't you, Luna-Bug?"

Luna got right in his face. "I don't have bugs!"

He leaned in close and picked a speck of something from one of the flowers on her hat.

"Gross! It's a bug! They're crawling all over you!" He jumped back and laughed like a donkey, showing off his squiggly metal teeth.

"Don't talk to her that way!" I said.

"Come on, Tiger." Luna grabbed my arm. "We're late. Let's go."

"Your name's Tiger?" Cooper snorted. "What's your last name? Lion?"

"It's Tiger Brooks," I said.

"This is too good," he howled. "Luna-Bug has a friend, and his name is Tiger! Let me see your spots, Tiger."

"Leopards have spots," I pointed out. "Tigers have stripes."

I checked my Batman watch. We had five minutes to get to Viola's.

"If you hang out with Luna, you'll get

Luna-Bug germs!" Cooper warned.

He let out another one of his donkey laughs. I felt bad for Luna. I had only known her for a week, since we moved into the neighborhood. She was a major chatterbox and did have some strange habits, but one thing was for sure: She was a nice person.

"Who are you to laugh at her?" I said to Cooper. "Your mouth looks like a circuit board."

From the stupid look that flashed across Cooper's face, I knew he had no idea what a circuit board was. Being a science guy, I've known about circuit boards ever since I took my first one apart. That was before I even got to kindergarten.

Cooper moved closer, blocking our way into Viola's yard. To my surprise, Luna sprang into action. She yanked off her hat. With her long black hair flying, she shoved the flowers in Cooper's face.

"Buggy-buggy-buggy-buggy!" she screamed at him.

He jumped back, pawing at his face and yelled, "Get 'em off me!"

Luna grabbed my arm and said, "Run like the wind!"

We pushed on Viola's creaky gate and ran up the overgrown path to the spidery door. I slammed the paintbrush door knocker like my life depended on it. Inside, we heard running hoofsteps. I could hear a voice saying, "No, Madame! It's too dangerous! I won't let you go!"

I looked back. Cooper had figured out the bugs were all in his mind and was shoving the squeaky gate open to come after us.

My heart was racing. I pounded the door knocker again.

Suddenly, the door swung open, and I was face-to-face with a bright orange pig. He looked frazzled and his bow tie was crooked.

"Chives," I said. "Is everything okay?"

He pulled Luna and me inside and slammed the door.

"We must hurry," he whispered. "We don't have a minute to lose."

CHAPTER 2

I could tell something was wrong. Chives was Viola Dots's butler, and he took his job very seriously. He was a formal kind of pig, not the kind to go around with his bow tie crooked.

"Come at once," Chives said, breathing hard. "Madame Dots is on a dangerous course of action, and she won't take no for an answer."

"Okay, but there's a kid outside following us," I told Chives.

Quickly, he opened the door a crack and looked out.

"I've seen that boy many times," he said, frowning. "He's a scoundrel and a bully. Like all bullies, he's a coward. He'll get frightened and run away."

"Why would he run away?"

"All the kids in the neighborhood are scared of Viola Dots," Luna explained. "They think she's a crazy old witch."

"Chives!" Viola's shrill voice drifted in from the living room. "What's taking so long? I need you! My bustle won't snap!"

"What's a *bustle*?" Luna asked.

"You'll see soon enough," Chives answered.

He headed quickly into the living room, and we followed.

"Don't just stand there like statues!" Viola barked without looking up. "Come in."

She was bent over and fiddling with something under her dress. I could see her legs, which were as white as cotton. My eyes decided to look away. Luckily, they found their way to the painting in the golden frame.

It was the same painting Chives and I had put there the week before. It showed a park by a river. People dressed in old-fashioned fancy clothes were strolling and relaxing. There were kids and dogs and sailboats, and even a monkey. I'm not much of an art person, but even I could tell it was a special painting.

"That painting is called *A Sunday Afternoon on the Island of La Grande Jatte*," Chives whispered. "That's in Paris, you know. Quite the masterpiece. The original was painted by Georges Seurat in 1884."

"This is no time for an art lesson, Chives," Viola snarled. "The clock is ticking. We have precisely two minutes before it strikes four."

It hit me that Viola was dressed just like the woman in the painting. She was wearing a fancy, old-fashioned gray dress that stuck way out in back. On her head was a black hat covered in red flowers. She even had an umbrella.

"I'm ready," she said, adjusting the back of her dress.

"You're not going with us, are you?" I asked her. I know that was a rude thing to say, but I couldn't help it. Having Viola along would ruin the fun.

"Indeed I am," she said. "I finally got this

bustle on, no thanks to my pig butler."

So that's what a bustle was. A pillow kind of thing that you put under your dress to make your butt stick out.

"Wow, you look amazing, Mrs. Dots," Luna said, running up to her. "I love your clothes. Can I borrow some of this stuff for dress up?"

"Certainly not!" Viola gave one final tug to her rump pillow.

"Mrs. Dots, no offense, but why do you want your butt to look big?" I asked.

"*Tsk*," Chives said. "Mind your manners, Master Tiger. That's not a question one asks a lady."

"It's quite rude," Viola agreed, "but it's an intelligent question. I always answer intelligent questions. Look at the painting carefully, young man. You'll notice that many of the ladies are wearing bustles. It was the fashion back then."

I studied the picture. It was true, especially for the tall woman in front. Her butt was the size of a small planet. My eyes drifted down to the clock on the bottom of the frame.

Oh no.

I checked my Batman watch, just to be sure. It said 3:59. This was no time to be standing around talking about rear ends.

"We have to get ready!" I cried. "It's almost here—the hour of power!"

It was approaching fast—the hour when the painting in the fantastic frame would swallow us up into its world, with only an hour to get home again.

Viola hurried to the painting and stood directly in front of it. "I'm going to go in with you children," she declared.

"Madame, it's too dangerous," Chives said. "Remember your advanced age."

"Nonsense, Chives! David is lost inside that frame. He's spent years drifting from painting to painting. He is my only son. I must bring him home."

"I understand how you feel, Mrs. Dots," Luna said. "But we promised you last week that we would help you find David. And we will."

"We're strong," I said. "We can travel into the painting. Please don't risk your life."

"Let me remind you children that you saw David last week in the jungle painting," Viola said, "yet you failed to bring him back.

So now I must try. I'm going with you to convince David to come home."

As Viola spoke, I heard a loud ticktock and saw the big hand on the clock strike twelve. It was four o'clock exactly. The hour of power was about to begin. Would the room suddenly start to shake? Would I be knocked off my feet and swept away? I wasn't sure. My heart raced as I waited for something big to happen.

Immediately, I noticed faraway sounds drifting into the room. First came the sound

of water, maybe a river lapping at the shores. *Splish, splash, splish, splash.* Then came a dog barking. *Arf, arf, arf.* I heard laughter, followed by the pitter-patter of footsteps on a soft surface.

Nothing sounded normal. It was as if the sounds were trying to squeeze into the giant living room through a very small hole.

"This is it!" Viola said. "The hour of power."

With a wild look in her eye, she grabbed both of Luna's hands and pulled her toward the painting.

"Here we come, David!" she cried.

We heard a rip, like paper being torn in two. Then I saw it: a small hole in the bottom of the painting, right next to the black dog. The barking grew louder. *ARF,*

ARF, ARF! The water lapped closer and closer. *SPLISH, SPLASH. SPLISH, SPLASH.* The footsteps echoed in my ears. A woman laughed loudly.

I felt myself being tugged toward the golden frame, as if some invisible force was pulling me into the painting. Luna was next to me, with Viola's hands still clutching hers tightly.

"Let go of her hands, Luna!" I cried. "She shouldn't come with us."

"I can't," Luna called back. "She's too strong."

Nothing could be done to stop us. It was happening. The painting was opening up.

"I can feel it!" Viola screamed. "The painting is pulling me in!"

She was right. Within seconds, the three

of us were nose to nose with the painting, staring at the French people parading around the island in their fancy clothes.

Up close, I noticed that all the people in the painting were made of small dots of color. In fact, everything in the scene was made of dots. Nothing was solid. The people, the boats, the trees, and the animals were all made with tiny spots of paint, blurring together to make one big picture.

The hole in the painting grew wider and wider. Luna was the first to get pulled in. I saw her head disappear into the opening. Viola Dots never let go of Luna's hands. Her head and her shoulders followed Luna into the painting. From inside, I heard her scream with terror and joy.

Just as the rest of her body was about to slip through the hole, her progress stopped. Her butt couldn't squeeze through. She was stuck halfway into the painting and halfway out, with her legs kicking and squirming in the living room.

"Somebody push my bustle," she shouted. "It's stuck."

"I won't do it, Madame!" Chives squealed.

"Chives, I order you to do it!" Viola hollered back.

"Beg your pardon, Madame, but I must refuse!"

With that, Chives reached out and locked his stubby legs around Mrs. Dots.

"One . . . two . . . three . . . ," he yelled.

He yanked so hard it seemed like he might tear Viola's legs off altogether, but she didn't seem to be budging. Then suddenly, there was a loud pop, followed by a gust of wind. When I looked up, I saw Viola flying out of the painting and back into the living room. Before I could figure out what had

happened, I was pulled like a magnet into
the hole she had left empty.

"Tiger, let me go back in!" Viola called.
"Stop right now!"

"I can't," I called as I was whooshed into the painting. "The force is too strong."

"Then promise me you'll look everywhere for David!" Viola shouted after me. "Tell him to come home."

Suddenly, everything grew dim. I began falling fast, dropping head over heels down a dark tunnel. I felt the wind whipping through my hair. I looked around for Luna. I could see her somersaulting down what looked like a flight of golden stairs. I closed my eyes and felt myself spinning. Dots of color swirled in my mind, and the real world seemed to melt away.

"Tiger," I heard Luna call. "Prepare for landing!"

It was the last thing I heard as I tumbled through time and space into another world.

CHAPTER 3

When I opened my eyes, I saw a body of water rushing toward us. We had missed the island and were going to land in the river! I had just enough time to take a deep breath before I fell headfirst into the freezing water.

"Luna!" I called, coming up for air. "Where are you?"

I saw her head pop out of the water.

"I'm okay," she said. "Let's get to shore."

We weren't far from the island. We swam by some people in a rowboat who were speaking a foreign language. They gave us strange looks. We just waved like it was a totally normal thing for a couple of American kids to land in their river. They paddled on, and we pulled ourselves onto the bank. We came ashore at exactly the spot where the painting had ripped open—right next to the umbrella woman with the bustle.

"Why is she holding an umbrella?" Luna whispered. "It's not even raining."

"I think she wants to keep the sun off her giant butt," I said.

Luna laughed. "I like you, Tiger."

I thought about telling her I liked her, too, but I was a little embarrassed to blurt it out.

I'm not like Luna. I can't just go around being all lovey-dovey.

We crawled onto the grass, dripping wet. "You wait here," I said to Luna. "I'll search around to see if I can find David. He's got to be here somewhere."

"I'm coming with you," Luna said.

Of course she was. Luna Lopez wasn't the kind of girl who would be happy staying behind.

The island was crowded with people. Everyone was relaxing in the sun or the shade, having a good time. Some were picking flowers, some were strolling by the shore. A man with big arms was lying on the grass smoking a long pipe.

"If he lived in the twenty-first century, he'd know that smoking that thing is going to make him sick," Luna said.

The man may have heard us whispering, because he turned around and shot a sour glance in our direction. We ducked behind a bush.

"We're safe here," I said.

"Not so fast, Tiger." Luna pointed to something behind me. "I think you're going to take that back."

When I turned around, I was face-to-face with a monkey whose long tail started to twitch when he spotted us. He opened his mouth and let out a piercing shriek. He wasn't that big, but he had sharp teeth and nasty little claws.

I don't speak monkey, but if I did, I'd bet he was saying, "Get out of here or I'm going to jump on your head."

"Nice monkey," Luna said, and gave him her best smile.

"Don't smile, Luna."

"Why not?"

"Because monkeys think you're making a threat when you smiiiii . . ."

The monkey opened his mouth wide and showed us his teeth.

"You just have to let him know you're not afraid," Luna said. "I saw that on the Animal Channel."

Luna put up her hand like she was going to give the monkey a high five. He reached for it, but she pulled her hand away fast.

"Too slow, Joe," she said with a laugh.

"That's a funny thing we say in the future, which is where we're from."

The monkey let out another fierce screech.

"So much for TV," Luna said.

The monkey jumped onto the woman's bustle, took aim, and dove straight for us. We took off so fast, we didn't really look where we were going. We ran right through a woman's lovely picnic, squashing her bread and cheese. She shook her finger at me and yelled something.

"Tell her I'm sorry," I shouted to Luna. "You speak Spanish."

"We're in a painting of *Paris*," Luna yelled. "Which is in France, where people speak French."

I was going so fast, I ran right into a little

girl in a white dress and knocked her off her feet.

"*Maman!*" she cried.

But her mama was busy, smacking me with her red umbrella. The little girl ran and hid in her mom's skirt, just like Maggie does with my mom when she's having one of her four-year-old scared attacks. That gave Luna a chance to grab the umbrella from the woman's hands.

"Back off," she called, holding the umbrella out in front of her like a sword. She looked like she was right out of one of those old pirate movies you see on TV. She spun around, pointing the umbrella at the crowd that was gathering.

"I can take you," she told the people. That wasn't far from the truth. She was tough.

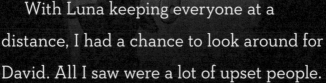

With Luna keeping everyone at a
distance, I had a chance to look around for
David. All I saw were a lot of upset people.

Most everyone had left their picnics, leaving the dogs and the monkey to grab their food. Our arrival had turned their lovely, peaceful afternoon into a real mess.

"Do you see David?" Luna asked. "I can't hold this umbrella forever."

I looked hard. I saw a woman fishing in the river, and some kids chasing one another. There was a couple kissing in the distance, and another couple getting in a rowboat.

Wait a minute. Back up, Tiger. That couple in the rowboat!

I squinted to get a closer look. I could see a blond girl wearing a straw hat with a big white bow. Helping her into the boat was a boy of about thirteen, with brown hair and a ruffled shirt. I couldn't see his

face clearly from where I
was standing. Could it
be David? He
was dressed
like a French
kid, but that
didn't mean
anything. Clothes were just clothes.

I jumped up and started shouting at him.

"David!" I yelled. "It's me, Tiger."

The boy looked over at me and paused
for a second. I yelled again.

"Luna's here, too," I shouted. "Your mom
sent us to find you!"

He took another few seconds to study
me, then the boy turned and got into the
boat. Without so much as a wave, he picked
up the oars and quickly rowed away.

CHAPTER 4

Luna was swinging the red umbrella at the puzzled crowd that had gathered around her.

"Just keep your distance, folks," she was saying, "and there won't be anything to worry about. We're here to look for a missing friend. He lives in your painting. Oh, I know you don't think you're living in a painting, but you are."

"Luna," I whispered. "Be quiet for a minute."

"Do I have to? This is really fun. It's like I'm the star of my own movie."

"Cut it out and listen to me. I saw David. At least I think it was him."

Before she could answer, a whistle blew.

"Here comes trouble," Luna said. "Just like in the movies."

Two men in orange-and-gray uniforms were hurrying toward us. They were very small in the painting, but now they were as big as life.

"They must be the police!" I said. "Or the army."

"So?" Luna said, swinging her umbrella. "Let them come."

"Listen to me, Luna. We can't get caught by the police. What if they keep us here? Or throw us in jail?"

"We'll escape," Luna said, her eyes lighting up at the thought of it.

"And if we don't, we're stuck here forever," I reminded her. "Besides, we came here to find David. And if that kid I saw was David, he's left the island and is heading to the mainland."

"Why didn't you say so, Tiger? We have to follow him!"

Luna dropped the umbrella, and we ran toward the shore. We looked around to see if the soldiers were still following us. They had been stopped by the black dog that was barking and running in circles around them. The little girl in white had thrown herself on the ground. That gave us time to reach the sand.

I looked across the river. In the distance

I could see the little rowboat making its way to the city. The girl's straw hat looked like a yellow dot on the dark blue river.

"We're going to have to row across," Luna said.

"Two problems," I said. "Number one, I don't know how to row a boat. And number two, we don't *have* a boat."

"I'm an expert boat rower," Luna said. "My grandpa Arturo taught me. We always go fishing when I visit him in Mexico."

"Fine, problem number one is solved. But what about number two?"

It occurred to me that this was the second time today I had said the words *number two*. It was a good thing Maggie wasn't there to have a giggle attack.

Luna looked up and down the beach.

There was only one rowboat left on the sand, and an old man and his wife were just settling into it.

"Come with me," Luna said, and before I could ask why, she had practically reached the old man's boat.

"Hi," she said to him, in her lovey-dovey voice. "I'm Luna, and this is Tiger. We were wondering if we could give you guys a hand. People your age shouldn't have to row yourselves."

"They don't understand a word you're saying," I said.

"My grandma always says, '*Una imagen vale más que mil palabras*,'" she said.

"Great. Now that makes three of us who don't understand a word you're saying."

"It's simple, Tiger. It means *a picture is*

worth a thousand words.
Just watch."

Luna picked up a stick
and quickly drew
a picture in the
sand—a boy,
a girl, and
a boat. She
looked at the couple
and pointed to herself.

Suddenly the woman burst into a big
smile and said something to her husband in
French. His face lit up, too.

"*Ah . . . oui, oui,*" he said, and held out his
hand.

"Is he offering to row us across the
river?" I asked Luna.

"No, *we're* offering to row *them* across

the river. Help me shove off before those
army guys catch us."

Luna jumped into the boat. She picked
up the oars and dug them into the sandy
bank.

"Push, Tiger," she called. "Then hop in."

I pushed the boat into the river and
leaped in. I landed with such a thud, I
almost tipped us over into the water. Luna
started to pull the oars through the water.
She really did know how to row.

"Do you see David up ahead?" she
asked. Her back was facing the mainland.

I could see the place where his
rowboat had landed, a little dock next
to some factory buildings. But I couldn't
see any signs of him. I was afraid he had
disappeared into the city.

"Luna, can you row faster?" I asked.

She put her head down and dug the oars deep into the water. A wind was blowing, making it hard for her to gain speed.

I looked down at my Batman watch. It was already 4:15. That left us exactly forty-five minutes to reach the shore, find David, convince him to come back with us, and row back to the island. Everything in me said that was impossible, and growing more impossible with each stroke of the oars.

The hour of power was ticking by fast, and there was nothing we could do to slow it down.

CHAPTER 5

Luna did her best, and we reached the
riverbank in record speed. As we helped
the old man and his wife out of the boat,
I heard the clip-clop of a horse-drawn
carriage coming down the street. The driver
pulled to the side of the road. He climbed
down, greeted the old couple warmly, and
opened the carriage door for them. I figured
he was probably their driver.

Before they got into the carriage, they

held their hands out to offer us a ride.

"Thanks, anyway," I said. "But we don't know where we're going. We're hoping to find our friend, and we think he's somewhere around here."

They just looked at me with a blank expression on their faces.

"Remember what I told you, Tiger," Luna said. "Pictures, not words."

She went up to the couple, shook her head no, and gave each of them a hug and waved good-bye.

They didn't understand my words, but they sure got the picture from Luna. They got in their carriage, leaned out the window, and blew a kiss.

"Okay, here's the plan," I said to Luna. "We move the boat away from the dock and

hide it under that tree. Then it will be here
when we get back with David."

Luna and I waded into the water. We
dragged the rowboat to a nearby tree
and tied it up. But when we tried to make
our way back to shore, we ran into a big
problem. The water was thick with dirt, and
it didn't smell too fresh, either.

Every time we tried
to take a step,
our feet would
get stuck in the
squishy mud.

"Wait . . .
I think I hear
someone

coming," Luna said, holding very still for a
moment. She was right. There were voices,

kids' voices. "Maybe they can help get us out of this muck."

We called out for help and within a minute, a group of five or six kids turned a corner and came down to the riverbank.

"Bonjour! Bonjour!" one boy shouted. He sounded friendly. When I looked up at him, all I could see were two bare feet and a dirty face.

He waded into the water and stuck out his hand to me. Another boy helped Luna. When we were both out, their friends gathered around us in a circle. There were six kids dressed in dirty rags and filthy caps.

They all started to say *bonjour* and a bunch of other French words I didn't understand.

It didn't take long for them to realize that neither of us could speak a word of French. We just kept repeating *bonjour*. Then we'd slap our chests and say our names. They didn't mind that we couldn't speak their language. They were excited to meet us.

The boy who had pulled me out of the river threw his arm around my shoulder. He was a head taller than me. I was pretty sure his name was Marcel. At least, that's what he kept saying every time he slapped his chest.

"*Américain?*" he asked.

There was a word I recognized.

"Yes," I said, nodding. "Tiger."

"*Américain, Américain!*" he said, poking his friends to let them know.

"Tiger, *Américain*," they all chanted.

"And this is Luna," I said, pointing to her.

"Luna, *Américaine*!" they cheered.

"I'm going to ask them where we can find David," Luna told me.

"What are the chances they know?"

"An American kid their age would stand out. It's worth a shot," Luna reasoned.

"How are you going to ask them? They won't understand you."

"Pictures, not words," Luna reminded me. "Just like Grandma says."

She turned to Marcel.

"David?" she asked. She held her hand above her head to show she was talking about someone taller than her. "David?"

"Ah . . . David," Marcel repeated. Then he pointed up the street. Luna broke into a smile.

"See, Tiger?" she said. "Don't be so negative. He's going to take us right to him."

Surrounded by our new group of friends, we turned a corner and headed up the cobblestone road. As we climbed the hill, we passed several factories. I could see shops and small houses up ahead. Marcel was taking us to that neighborhood. I was sure David was there, probably walking the girl in the straw hat home right about now.

If we could find David in the next few minutes, we had a good chance of making it back to the island by five o'clock. For the first time since Luna and I had landed, I took a deep breath. I thought of Viola Dots finally getting to see her long-lost son, and a feeling of happiness swept over me.

"Marcel," I said, throwing my arm around his shoulder. I couldn't quite reach his shoulder, but I stood on my tiptoes and did the best I could. "Luna and I really appreciate your help."

Marcel didn't answer. Or even seem to care. He was looking at a man coming out of one of the factory doors. He was a very rich-looking man, wearing a top hat and bow tie, just like Chives.

All the kids had slowed and were watching the man walk down the cobblestone street. They became very quiet. Too quiet.

The man stopped walking. Stroking his gray whiskers, he pulled a shiny gold watch from his vest pocket.

Marcel whispered something in French

to me, pointing to the man.

"Sorry, Marcel," I said. "I don't understand."

When he heard my voice, the man looked up. Without any warning, Marcel pushed my back hard. I lost my balance and staggered several steps to keep from falling. Before I realized what was happening, I had smashed right into the man with the pocket watch.

I slammed into him so hard, I knocked him down. While he was on the ground, Marcel and the street kids charged him, whooping and laughing. Then they grabbed his pocket watch and raced up the road! It all happened very fast. I suddenly realized that they had already done this many times before.

Marcel stayed behind an extra second so he could squash the man's top hat under his foot, just like Cooper Starr had smashed my plastic cup. Then he fled with the rest of his friends.

"Tiger, what happened?" Luna called as she ran to me. "Where are the others? Why did you knock this man over?"

What could I say to her? That I had just helped Marcel and his friends rob a man?

I felt terrible. I reached out and picked up his flattened top hat. I popped it back out to its original shape and offered it to him. He batted it away.

"*Gendarmes!*" he called at the top of his voice.

You didn't have to speak French to know that he was calling for help. My heart started to race. I had no idea what to do.

We heard voices in the distance, followed by whistles and the clatter of hooves. Marcel and his pack darted around the corner and ran past us. Following them were two policemen on horseback.

The street kids swarmed around Luna and me. Grabbing our arms, they swept us up with them. The police galloped after us. Marcel ran next to me.

"Tiger, *Américain*," he called.

Then he tossed me the gold watch. I'm a baseball player. You throw me anything, I'm going to catch it. Without thinking, I reached out and caught the watch in midair. Marcel took off in a burst of speed. He and his pals scattered, disappearing into side alleys. Only Luna and I were left on the street. The river was to our left. Buildings to our right.

"We're trapped!" I shouted.

"Let's swim for it," Luna said.

But it was too late.

We were surrounded by the police.

CHAPTER 6

The policemen carried old-fashioned prison irons in their saddlebags. After they caught us, they got them out and handcuffed us. I felt the thick iron bracelet clamp around my wrist. I heard another one clamp. That was Luna's. She started to cry. And to be honest, I did, too.

I was still clutching the gold watch in my hand. One of the policemen took it from me. He let it dangle from the chain.

"Ooh-la-la," the policeman said when
the shiny watch caught the sunlight. Like
most of the police, he had a complicated
mustache. It was as skinny as he was.

His partner, a gray-haired man with a big
belly, wagged his finger at me.

"Tsk-tsk-tsk," he said.

"That's not mine," I tried to explain.

He shrugged his shoulders. I pointed to the gentleman who had been robbed.

"Ask him," I said. "He'll tell you I didn't steal his watch. Marcel did it."

"Tiger, it's no use trying to explain," Luna whispered. "They don't understand you."

"Can't you draw a picture for them?" I begged. "You know, like your grandma tells you to."

"Not with these handcuffs on." Luna shook her head sadly. The skinny policeman got right in my face and started firing questions at me in French.

"It's not mine," I kept yelling. "I didn't steal it."

"Try not to yell at him," Luna suggested. "My grandma always says it's not what you say that matters, it's how you say it."

"Your grandmother sure has a lot of advice," I snapped. "Maybe she should give it a rest."

Luna looked hurt.

"I'm sorry, Luna," I said with a sigh. "I'm scared. And I don't like being accused of stuff I didn't do."

The policeman kept at it, asking one question after another right into my face. He must have eaten a garlic sandwich for lunch, with a side of garlic. His breath smelled like a three-day-old sausage.

Suddenly, his gray-haired partner put his

finger to his lips and looked around.

"Shhhhh," he said. We all listened. We heard footsteps from across the street.

The older officer ran off in the direction of the footsteps. I was surprised at how fast he could go. He disappeared behind a building. Not more than a minute later, he appeared, pulling a kid by the ear. It was Marcel!

"That's him!" I shouted to Mr. Garlic Breath. "He's the thief, not me."

Marcel stared at me with angry eyes. When the police weren't looking, he clenched his hand into a fist as if he were going to punch me. I knew what that meant in any language—keep your mouth shut.

The policemen put Marcel in handcuffs, too. Then they chained all three of us to the horses. We had to walk through the narrow lanes of shops to the station. People leaned out from their upstairs windows and shouted at us. Marcel smirked at them and shouted back. Not me. I was so embarrassed, I wanted to sink into a hole and disappear.

"What time is it, Tiger?" Luna whispered.

I wiped a thick layer of mud from my Batman watch. Good thing Batman is so tough. My watch was waterproof, mudproof, and even other dimension-proof. Batman kept going, no matter what.

And that was a problem. The time was

4:35. We had twenty-five minutes to find David and get back to the island.

"We'll never make it," Luna said. "We'll be stuck in here forever. I'll never see my parents or grandparents again. I'll never have another *horchata*. And what's going to happen to my kitty, Loco? She gets so nervous without me."

"*Silence!*" a policeman barked.

"I won't be quiet!" Luna shouted. "We don't belong here. We're from the future. Don't you know that you're in a painting? None of this is real!"

But it was real. We were in handcuffs in a foreign country, far from home. Accused of a crime we didn't do. With no one to help us.

The chains around me were suddenly very heavy, and I felt like I was sinking.

CHAPTER 7

The prison door clanged shut. And just like that, Luna and I were locked inside.

After marching us through the street to the station, the police put Luna, Marcel, and me into a jail cell. There were about ten other kids in different cells on either side of us. Marcel seemed to know them all.

I squatted behind the prison bars, looking at my Batman watch. Luna yelled and screamed at the guard. Then she got really chatty with him. But nothing was working.

A new guard walked by and nudged me with a baton. He handed me something wrapped up in a dirty piece of cloth. A thick chunk of crunchy bread was inside. He gave one to Luna and Marcel, too, then went on to the next cell block.

I took a bite. Before I could take a second bite, Marcel snatched the bread from me and wolfed it down. I got so angry, I felt like I was going to explode. And I did. I shoved Marcel as hard as I could with both arms.

I didn't do *any* damage. Marcel grabbed me by the wrist. I thought he was going to twist my arm, but he didn't. Instead, he held my wrist to his face. He was looking at my

Batman watch. I could tell that he'd never seen anything like it.

He asked me a question in French. What did he want to know? I couldn't tell. He repeated the question. I shrugged.

"It's Batman! Everyone knows that." The answer came from a kid standing on the free side of the bars. "The Caped Crusader of Gotham. He's the best superhero ever."

I thought I knew that voice. No, I was *sure* I knew that voice.

It was David! He was wearing brown pants and a ruffled shirt.

The guard undid David's irons, slid open the bars, and tossed him into our cell. Luna ran to him and gave him one of her huge hugs—the Luna Special.

"David, you have no idea how good it is to see you," she cried.

"Although it'd be better to run into each other in a place without bars," I added.

David laughed out loud, like he wasn't bothered a bit.

"So it *was* you I saw getting into the rowboat," I said. "Why didn't you answer when I called?"

"I was on a date," David said. "With Celeste. She's the most beautiful girl in the whole painting. This life sure beats the jungle, wouldn't you say?"

The last time we had seen David, he was living in a jungle painting. He was so hairy and dirty then that he looked like half boy, half animal. This time, he was all cleaned up. One other thing was different about him, too. He could speak French. He must have picked it up from living in all those different French paintings.

"Your mom misses you so much," Luna said to him. "She wants you to come home."

"I know," David said. "I miss her, too, but I'd miss Celeste more."

He laughed again, and the sound of it filled the whole prison cell.

David looked around and waved hello to the kids in the other cells. He even said *bonjour* to Marcel, and the two of them talked like they were old pals.

"Marcel says they picked you up for stealing a gold watch," he said, turning to us. "My mother wouldn't be happy about that."

"We didn't steal anything," I said. "Marcel set us up. He stole the watch."

"Marcel will do that," David said. "He's a regular in this establishment."

"He's a bully and a scoundrel," I said, remembering that Chives had used those very words to describe Cooper Starr.

"Scoundrel? Nice vocabulary, buddy," David said, punching me lightly in the arm. "Where'd you learn a fancy word like that?"

"From your mother's orange pig butler."

"That sounds like something Mother would have," he said with a laugh. "Well, you've got to understand that Marcel has had a hard life. His parents abandoned him. He's been on the streets his whole life, or here in prison."

"Why are you in here?" Luna asked.

"When I was dropping Celeste off at her house, I saw the police taking you in chains. I knew they were bringing you here. I stole a piece of bread so they'd throw me in jail, too. I thought maybe you'd need my help."

"We need major help," I said. "Time is running out. If we're not back at five, we're stuck here forever."

"I know," David said. "The window is closing, and we have to get you out of here fast. I have an idea, but I'm going to need Marcel's help. That won't be easy. I happen to know that he hates helping others."

"Tell him we're from the twenty-first

century," Luna suggested. "And that we need to get back to the future."

"I've found that that doesn't usually work," David answered.

We were wasting time. I was desperate. "Tell him we'll give him anything. Anything he wants."

"Now there's something that could work," David said.

He went to Marcel and huddled with him. Then he came back to us.

"He'll help us, but only if you give him your Batman watch," David said.

"My watch? But it's special. My uncle Cole gave it to me for my tenth birthday, and he's my favorite uncle."

"Then I hope you like bread and water," David said. "Because that's what they feed you in French prisons."

"I think I can get Marcel to help us," Luna said. "I'm going to talk to him."

"He doesn't speak English," David reminded her.

"That won't bother her," I said. "Her grandma taught her to communicate in pictures."

"She also says that if people look deep in your eyes, they can tell what you're feeling," Luna said. "I'm going to look into Marcel's eyes and let him know I'm sorry he's had such a hard life. I bet that will soften him up."

Luna walked over to Marcel, wrapped her arms

around him, and gave him a great big hug. She looked him deep in the eyes. He seemed to like it. They walked back over to us, and Marcel said something in French to David.

"It worked, didn't it?" Luna said. "What did he say?"

"He says thanks for the hug," David said.

"I knew it!" Luna shouted.

"And that he still wants the watch," David added.

Luna looked crushed.

"Nice try," David said to her. "But sometimes a jerk is a jerk, no matter what you do." Then, turning to me, he said, "Looks like it's up to you, Tiger. What's it going to be?"

I looked at my Batman watch, with its

cool light-up face. It was my favorite thing that I owned. I'd probably be fifty before I'd ever get another one.

Then I looked at Luna. She was biting her lower lip, waiting for my decision. It was a hard choice, one that I wished I didn't have to make.

CHAPTER 8

"Decision time, buddy," David said, tapping his foot. "We're wasting time here."

I thought about the day my uncle Cole gave me the Batman watch. He's a huge Batman fan, too. We were at a Dodgers game, and he pulled the box out of his backpack and handed it to me, all wrapped up in comic-book wrapping paper. I was so excited. Afterward, we ate hot dogs with chili. That was a great day.

I sighed, knowing what I had to
do. I took one last look at my Batman
watch and unfastened the strap.

"So long, Batman," I said, handing the watch to Marcel. "You'll just have to fight crime without me."

"That was a good decision," David said as Marcel strapped on the watch and danced around the cell.

"Thanks, Tiger," Luna said. "If we get home . . . I mean . . . *when* we get home, I'll make you something special to replace that. I know how to make this cool friendship bracelet out of leather and seashells."

David laughed.

"Now there's a reason to hurry home," he said. "Come on, let's get to work."

Quickly, he described his plan to us.

"It's risky," he said, "but it's our best shot. Let me just tell Marcel what to do."

He spoke quickly to Marcel, who

listened and nodded without ever looking up from the watch on his wrist.

"Okay," David said. "Are you guys ready?"

"Just one question," I said to him. "If it works and we get out of jail, you are coming back with us, aren't you?"

"Maybe." He shrugged.

"But you have to," Luna said.

"I don't have to do anything," David answered. "That's why I like it here in the world of art. I'm not just a thirteen-year-old kid. I'm free. No bedtime. No piano practice. No math homework."

"But what about your mom?" Luna said. "Do you know she does a new painting every week, hoping that you'll be in it?"

"All right, Luna, I'll think about it." David

glanced over at my watch on Marcel's arm. "Look, it's already 4:45. We've got to move."

David gave Marcel a hand signal. Marcel nodded, cracked his knuckles, and then suddenly charged David. If I hadn't known better, I would have thought they really hated each other. They were fighting like real enemies. Throwing punches, taking punches, pulling hair, hitting low. David even let Marcel give him a bloody nose so everything would look real.

The kids in the cells around us started hooting and hollering and rattling the bars. The guard on duty came running. He swung open the bars and barged into our cell to break up the fight.

"Run!" David yelled to us.

Luna and I ran out to freedom. Marcel and David bolted, too, just a step behind us. David swung the bars closed, locking the guard in the cell. Marcel showed us that he had pickpocketed the guard's key.

"Au revoir, les Américains!" Marcel called out, then hurried to let his friends out of the other cells.

The three of us crept down the hall. Quietly, we snuck out the back door of the station. We were halfway down the alley when we finally heard an alarm bell go off.

"They'll be coming after us now," David said.

"Which way is the river?" I whispered.

"That way." David pointed. "Time is really tight."

"Then we'll run like the wind," Luna said.

"We need something faster than wind,"
I said. "The fastest things they have here
are horses."

"There's one over there," David said.
It was a police horse, drinking at a trough
by the station. "I can ride any horse. My
mother made me take lessons."

"We can't get all three of us on one
horse," Luna said.

If I could get my brain to work, maybe I
could come up with an invention that would
help us get to the river as fast as possible.

*Think, Tiger. Be a science guy. Imagine
you're Thomas Edison. Or Alexander
Graham Bell. Or Henry Ford.*

I looked around desperately and spotted
an old wooden fruit cart on the side of the
alley. It was basically a wheelbarrow with

a lot of cherry
pits and banana
peels in it. It had
only one wheel.
But maybe I

could rig something up and tie it to the
horse.

"You get the horse," I called to David.
"I'll make a chariot."

David dashed to the horse and leaped on
its back in one move.

Meanwhile, Luna helped me shove the
broken-down cart into the street. It was
very rickety. It was made to haul around
fruit, not two ten-year-olds. But our only
hope was to try it.

I looked around for rope to make the
rigging. We had nothing. Luna was starting

to panic, but I stayed calm. I think best in tight spots, and besides, the answer was staring right at me.

Underpants!

Right next to us, there was a clothesline with a row of men's underpants drying on the line. I felt bad for the poor guy who'd have to wear damp undies for a while, but not bad enough to stop me from yanking them off the line.

I pulled down the clothesline. It gave me more than enough rope. Quickly, I tied the rope around the fruit cart's handles—with a bowline knot, in case you care about knots. David brought the horse over to us, and I tossed the rope to him. He tied his end around the saddle. Luna and I jumped in the cart.

The horse reared up on its hind legs. The cart almost tipped completely over.

"We're falling out!" Luna cried.

David dug his heels into the horse's sides. The horse reared one more time, and then took off.

"Try to hang on," I called to Luna.

"I don't think I can!" she screamed.

There was no time to answer her. We were already flying down the alley, speeding on one shaky wheel across the bumpy streets of Paris.

CHAPTER 9

The cart bounced and rattled over every single cobblestone. David weaved in and out of carriages and pedestrians. Every time he turned the horse even slightly, Luna and I nearly toppled out the side. I could see little fibers of the clothesline starting to snap off. We were hanging on by a thread.

People were diving out of the way. The police were chasing us, blowing their whistles.

"Hee ya!" David yelled, spurring the horse on with his heels. The horse shifted into light speed. The air was coming at me so fast, I could barely open my eyes.

But I could smell. And I'm not kidding, I smelled water. Stinky water.

As David turned the corner, I caught sight of the river.

"Over there, by the tree," I hollered. "We left a boat there."

David galloped up to the bank and pulled on the reins sharply. We stopped so suddenly that Luna and I flew out of the cart. We landed in the squishy mud.

The good news was that our boat was still there, tied to the tree. The bad news was that four policemen had turned the corner and were galloping toward us.

Luna and I dove into the water and made our way over to the boat.

"Come on, David!" I cried out.

"I'll lead the police away," he called out. "You guys just get back to the island."

"No!" Luna and I both yelled.

"I'll come with you another time. Tell my mom to paint something American. I'll need a hamburger and fries after this!"

With that, he kicked his horse and cried out, "Hee ya!" The horse reared back on its hind legs and galloped into the streets of Paris. The policemen followed him. David turned back and waved to us. He looked like he was having the time of his life.

Luna and I jumped into the boat. She picked up the oars and started to row. I flipped over onto my stomach and put my hands in the water, paddling in the same rhythm as Luna. I'm not sure how much it helped, but at least I was doing something. The wind was blowing and there were dark clouds overhead.

"I think it's going to rain," Luna called out. There was a little panic in her voice.

"No, it won't," I called back. "It's not raining in the painting. The sun is out."

The island was not far now. As I looked at it, suddenly it seemed like it was made of little dots of color, just like the painting. I blinked hard and looked again. The river, the sky, the grass—everything was a swirl of tiny dancing spots of paint. I hadn't noticed any of that when we first landed. I guess I was too focused on finding David.

The current was very strong, and my

arms were burning from paddling. I pulled them out of the water and shook them—and that was when I noticed that my skin looked strange, too. My arms were covered in spots! Pink and gray and brown spots that blended together to look like skin.

I remembered what David had said in our prison cell. *The window is closing.* Was that what was happening? Was it five o'clock? Were we becoming part of the painting?

Out of habit, I looked down to check my Batman watch. It was gone. All I saw was my spotted arm. We reached shore and pulled the rowboat onto the sand.

"We're here," Luna panted. "Stand still and let's go home."

We stood perfectly still and waited. Nothing happened.

"Oh no!" she said. "Is it after five? Maybe we're too late!"

"Let's try going back to the exact spot where the painting ripped open," I said.

We crept over to the grass. There they all were, strolling and eating and relaxing, just like when we'd dropped into the painting.

"We can't freak anyone out this time," I whispered to Luna. "Everything else has to be the same as we found it."

"We'll cover ourselves with these," Luna suggested.

She handed me branches that had fallen from a tree. We threw them over us and scooted farther onto the grass, heading to where the black dog and the monkey were standing.

"This is the spot," I whispered. "I got a good look at it when Viola was kicking and screaming."

Luna and I crouched down next to the monkey and stood very still. The colors were swirling in my eyes. I smiled at Luna to show her I wasn't afraid.

"Tiger," she gasped. "Your face . . . it's covered in dots. Is mine, too?"

I didn't want to tell her that it was.

"Hold still," I said. "Maybe the dots will disappear as soon as we're home."

"But, Tiger," she cried. "What if they don't? What if . . ."

I didn't hear the rest. The world started to spin. I saw a monkey's razor-sharp claw reach out, one nanosecond away from slashing me.

Time froze. I felt myself fall backward, away from the island, out of that world.

Everything around me dissolved into tiny points of light. As darkness fell over me, it looked like glitter tossed up into the night sky.

CHAPTER 10

It's hard to describe what it's like to return
from the painting back into the real world.
I can only remember it in little bits and
pieces. A flash of color whirling in the
darkness. The smell of paint. The feeling of
climbing and falling at the same time.

The first thing I remember clearly is seeing
a hole with an orange snout peeking through.
Then I saw a black hat with red flowers. And
was that a gray bustle I was heading toward?

Yes. It was Viola and Chives, reaching out to us from the real world.

Luna and I catapulted out of the hole and into Viola's living room. I wish I had a video of the whole thing, because I'm sure that I did some gymnastic moves that I'll never be able to do again. Luna followed me, doing some pretty fantastic moves herself.

"Where's David?!" Viola asked the moment we hit the floor.

Luna reached up and touched her face.

"Mrs. Dots, do I have dots?" she asked.

"Of course you don't," Viola said. "Now stop talking nonsense and answer my question about David. Is he with you?"

"We saw him," I said, checking my own arms. They were dot-free, too.

"Where did you see him?" Viola asked. "Is he in the painting?"

"He's in Paris," I answered.

"Why is he there? Why isn't he here?"

She ran her hands over the entire surface of the painting, looking for the hole. But the painting had closed back up. It was the same as it had been before the hour of power.

"I'm sorry, Mrs. Dots," Luna said. "But—"

"But what? What did you do to him?"

"Madame, let them explain," Chives said. "Come, sit down."

He led her over to a couch. She tried to sit, but the bustle kept getting in the way. She ripped it off and threw it at the wall.

"David saved us," I told her. "We were being chased by the police, and he led them away from us."

"He saved you *last* week, too," Viola said. "You both require too much saving."

"He wants to come back," Luna said. "I know he does. He just couldn't make it this week."

Viola let out such a sad little moan. Luna walked over and sat down next to her on the sofa. I felt a hug coming on, and I wasn't wrong. Luna got really close to Viola and put out her arms. Viola slid away. It looked like the Luna Special wasn't going to work this time.

"I ask you to do one simple thing," Viola said, "and you can't do it."

"It wasn't easy in there," I said, pointing to the painting. "It might look all peaceful and friendly, but it was very dangerous. There were police and mean boys and, at the very end, we almost turned into dots ourselves."

Viola clutched her chest. "And what about David? Is he safe? Is he eating enough?"

"Yes," I said, "but he misses hamburgers and fries. He wants you to paint something American next time."

"Of course. Anything that will bring him closer to home. Anything at all."

"We'll try again, Mrs. Dots," Luna said. "We know how much you want him back."

"Tomorrow?" she asked.

"Whoa, not that soon," I said. "My head is still spinning from all that time travel."

But Viola wasn't listening.

"Hamburgers and fries," she was muttering. "Ah, I know just the thing."

She stood up and clapped her hands.

"Chives, fetch my painting supplies. Stretch a fresh canvas. And, of course, make me my tea, not too hot, but not too cold, either."

She barely even noticed when we left the house. We were very tired, so tired that we had both forgotten all about Cooper Starr.

But he hadn't forgotten about us.

Cooper was sitting alone on the curb by Viola's house. He looked bored, just tossing pebbles into a puddle by the curb. I wondered what he would think if he knew we had just had the most exciting adventure in the whole world.

"You know who Cooper reminds me of?" Luna said. "Marcel."

"No way. Marcel has brown hair and no braces."

"Not the way he looks, Tiger, but the way he acts. All tough on the outside.

But sad and alone on the inside."

I thought about that. It was Sunday at five o'clock. I was heading home to my family. Every Sunday, my dad cooks his amazing spaghetti and meatballs.
I wondered if anyone ever made spaghetti for Cooper.

"Maybe his life's hard, too, and he's sad like Marcel," Luna said. "I'm going to try to be kind to him."

"Can't hurt to try."

When we opened the creaky gate, Cooper sprang to his feet.

"Hi, Cooper," Luna said with a big smile. "You're looking very nice right now."

"Hello, loser," he answered. "How's your bugs?"

"On the other hand," Luna said, "like

David says, sometimes a jerk is just a jerk."

We laughed all the way back to our duplex.

When I got home, dinner was ready. We sat down at the kitchen table. My dad brought us each a plate of spaghetti and meatballs. Just as I was taking my first bite, I glanced out the kitchen window. In the shadows I saw Chives, peeking out at us through the curtains of Viola's house.

Maggie saw him, too.

"Look," she cried, jumping to her feet. "It's the orange pig!"

"No such thing, squirt," I said with a mouthful of meatball. Across the way, I saw the curtain close.

Maggie was so excited, she jumped up and knocked her plastic plate off the table. The spaghetti went splat, all over the kitchen floor.

"Oh well," my mom said. "I guess it's just another messy Sunday."

I laughed to myself. She had no idea how true that was!

ABOUT THE PAINTING

A Sunday Afternoon on the Island of La Grande Jatte by Georges Seurat

A Sunday Afternoon on the Island of La Grande Jatte is a large and beautiful oil painting by the French artist Georges Seurat. It's the size of a wall mural, measuring over six feet high and ten feet in length. The artist worked on the painting for two years before it was first exhibited in 1886. He continued to make changes to it for another three years after that.

The painting shows a Sunday afternoon scene on the island of La Grande Jatte. The island is in the Seine River, which flows through the middle of the city of Paris, France. In Seurat's day, the island was used as a public park for the people of Paris. They would go there by boat, then stroll and picnic and relax. You'll notice that in the painting, there are many different kinds of people: boaters, soldiers, children, women in fancy clothes, and men in top hats. There are forty-eight people, eight boats, three dogs, and one monkey—so much to look at and enjoy!

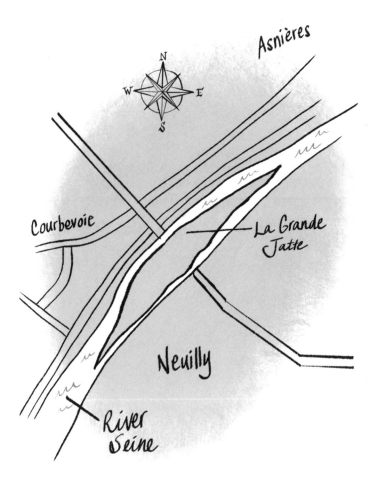

But what is most famous about this painting is the *way* it is painted—its technique. It uses a style called *pointillism*. Seurat did not invent the word, but he did invent the technique.

The traditional painters that came before Seurat used a *palette*, a flat surface on which they arranged and mixed colors. For instance, they might mix together red and white to make pink, or blue and red to make purple. Then they would take the paint from their palette and apply it to the canvas with brushstrokes or other kinds of marks.

But Seurat did something quite different. He applied small, separate dots of pure color to the canvas. The entire painting of *A Sunday Afternoon on the Island of La Grande Jatte*—every bit—is made up of tiny dots of pure color. It is our eyes and our brains that mix the colors together to form a new color. (By the way, this is also the way a computer screen works; the picture you see on the screen is made up of tiny pixels which your eyes put together to form an image.)

For example, if you look closely at the scene in the park, you can see that the trees are not just green. They are made of tiny dots of green and blue and brown and yellow and black. Each color is a separate dot. But when you stand back and look at the trees, your eyes blend the colors so that what you see is shades of green. Seurat was known as an artist-scientist because of the scientific way he chose and applied his colors.

Georges Seurat was born in 1859 in France. He went to art school, and then dropped out to join the army. He was twenty-five years old when he began painting *A Sunday Afternoon on the Island of La Grande Jatte*. He died when he was only thirty-one years old. His career as an artist was very short, yet he left behind one of the greatest art masterpieces of all time.

A Sunday Afternoon on the Island of La Grande Jatte hangs in the Art Institute of Chicago in Illinois.

ABOUT THE AUTHOR

Lin Oliver is the *New York Times* best-selling author of more than thirty books for young readers. She is also a film and television producer, having created shows for Nickelodeon, PBS, Disney Channel, and Fox. The cofounder and executive director of the Society of Children's Book Writers and Illustrators, she loves to hang out with children's book creators. Lin lives in Los Angeles, in the shadow of the Hollywood sign, but when she travels, she visits the great paintings of the world and imagines what it would be like to be inside the painting—so you might say she carries her own Fantastic Frame with her!

ABOUT THE ILLUSTRATOR

Samantha Kallis is a Los Angeles-based illustrator and visual development artist. Since graduating from Art Center College of Design in Pasadena, California, in 2010, her work has been featured in television, film, publishing, and galleries throughout the world. Samantha can be found most days on the porch of her periwinkle-blue Victorian cottage, where she lives with her husband and their two cats. More of her work can be seen on her website: www.samkallis.com.